Once upon a time there were

three billy goats called Gruff.

They ate grass all day long.

The Three Billy Goats Gruff

by Amelia Marshall and Karl West

FRANKLIN WATTS

LONDON·SYDNEY

Soon, there was no more grass left
in the field. The three Billy Goats Gruff
had eaten it all up!

"Look, there is lots of sweet green grass in the next field," said Big Billy Goat. "But we will have to cross the wooden bridge," said Middle Billy Goat. "A troll lives there who will eat us up," said Little Billy Goat.

Big Billy Goat smiled.

"Don't worry, I have a plan," he said.

Next day, Little Billy Goat went
to the bridge.

"Trip-Trap, Trip-trap," went his hooves
on the wood.

Out jumped the big, ugly troll.

"Who is that trip-trapping over my bridge?"

he roared.

"I am Little Billy Goat Gruff. I am going to eat the sweet green grass in the field."

"Oh no you are not," said the troll.
"I am going to eat you for breakfast."

"Oh no, don't eat me. Wait for
my brother, Middle Billy Goat Gruff.
He is much bigger than me,"
said Little Billy Goat.

"Then I will gobble him up!" said the troll.

Next, Middle Billy Goat went to the bridge.

Trip-Trap, Trip-trap, Trip-trap went

his hooves on the wood.

"Who is that trip-trapping over my bridge?" roared the troll.

"I am Middle Billy Goat Gruff. I am going to eat the sweet grass in the field."

"Oh no you're not. I am going to eat you for my lunch," roared the troll, rubbing his belly.

"Oh no, don't eat me. Wait for my brother, Big Billy Goat Gruff. He is much bigger than me," said Middle Billy Goat Gruff.

Then Big Billy Goat went to the bridge.

Trip-trap, Trip-trap, Trip-trap, Trip-trap

went his loud, heavy hooves on the wood.

"Who is that trip-trapping over my bridge?" roared the troll. "I'm going to eat you for my dinner!"

The troll jumped up onto the bridge.

He looked at Big Billy Goat Gruff.

He looked at the very, very big horns ...

Big Billy Goat lowered
his very, very big horns
and charged at the troll.

SPLASH!

Big Billy Goat knocked the big, ugly troll off the bridge and into the river below.

The Three Billy Goats enjoyed

the sweet green grass.

And they never saw the big, ugly troll again.

Story order

Look at these 5 pictures and captions.
Put the pictures in the right order
to retell the story.

1

The troll lands in the water!

2

Big Billy Goat crosses the bridge.

3

Middle Billy Goat crosses the bridge.

4

Little Billy Goat crosses the bridge.

5

The Billy Goats need to find more grass.

Independent Reading

This series is designed to provide an opportunity for your child to read on their own. These notes are written for you to help your child choose a book and to read it independently.

In school, your child's teacher will often be using reading books which have been banded to support the process of learning to read. Use the book band colour your child is reading in school to help you make a good choice. *The Three Billy Goats Gruff* is a good choice for children reading at Purple Band in their classroom to read independently.

The aim of independent reading is to read this book with ease, so that your child enjoys the story and relates it to their own experiences.

About the book

The Three Billy Goats need more fresh, green grass to eat. They must cross the bridge to the next field, but a hungry troll lies in wait.

Before reading

Help your child to learn how to make good choices by asking:
"Why did you choose this book? Why do you think you will enjoy it?"
Look at the cover together and ask: "What do you think the story will be about?" Ask your child to think of what they already know about the story context. Then ask your child to read the title aloud. Ask:
"What do you think is going to happen when the goats try to cross the bridge?"

Remind your child that they can sound out the letters to make a word if they get stuck.

Decide together whether your child will read the story independently or read it aloud to you.

During reading

Remind your child of what they know and what they can do independently. If reading aloud, support your child if they hesitate or ask for help by telling the word. If reading to themselves, remind your child that they can come and ask for your help if stuck.

After reading

Support comprehension by asking your child to tell you about the story. Use the story order puzzle to encourage your child to retell the story in the right sequence, in their own words. The correct sequence can be found on the next page.

Help your child think about the messages in the book that go beyond the story and ask: "Why does the troll want to stop the goats crossing the bridge? How do the goats manage to trick the troll?" Give your child a chance to respond to the story: "What was your favourite part and why? How do you think the troll felt in the end?"

Extending learning

Help your child understand the story structure by using the same sentence patterning and adding different elements. "Let's make up a new story about the Billy Goats Gruff. Who might they meet on the bridge this time? How else could they get across the bridge?"

In the classroom, your child's teacher may be teaching different kinds of sentences. There are many examples in this book that you could look at with your child, including statements, commands and questions. Find these together and point out how the end punctuation can help us decide what kind of sentence it is.

Franklin Watts
First published in Great Britain in 2022
by The Watts Publishing Group

Copyright © The Watts Publishing Group 2022

Series Editors: Jackie Hamley, Melanie Palmer and Grace Glendinning
Series Advisors and Development Editors: Dr Sue Bodman and Glen Franklin
Series Designers: Peter Scoulding and Cathryn Gilbert

A CIP catalogue record for this book is
available from the British Library.

ISBN 978 1 4451 8403 6 (hbk)
ISBN 978 1 4451 8404 3 (pbk)
ISBN 978 1 4451 8463 0 (library ebook)
ISBN 978 1 4451 8464 7(ebook)

Printed in China

Franklin Watts
An imprint of
Hachette Children's Group
Part of The Watts Publishing Group
Carmelite House
50 Victoria Embankment
London EC4Y 0DZ

An Hachette UK Company
www.hachette.co.uk

www.reading-champion.co.uk

FSC
www.fsc.org
MIX
Paper from
responsible sources
FSC® C104740

Answer to Story order: 5, 4, 3, 2, 1